W9-BHL-293

BLOODLINES

CONTROL UNDER FIRE

written by
M. Zachary Sherman

illustrated by
Fritz Casas

colored by
Marlon Ilagan

STONE ARCH BOOKS
a capstone imprint

DEDICATED TO THE MEN AND WOMEN
OF THE ARMED SERVICES

Bloodlines is published by Stone Arch Books
a Capstone imprint, 151 Good Counsel Drive,
P.O. Box 669 Mankato, Minnesota 56002
www.capstonepub.com Copyright © 2011 by
Stone Arch Books All rights reserved. No
part of this publication may be reproduced
in whole or in part, or stored in a retrieval
system, or transmitted in any form or by any
means, electronic, mechanical, photocopying,
recording, or otherwise, without written
permission of the publisher.

Cataloging-in-Publication Data is available on
the Library of Congress website.
ISBN: 978-1-4342-2561-0 (library binding)
ISBN: 978-1-4342-3100-0 (paperback)

Summary: Technology and air superiority
equals success in modern warfare. But even
during the War in Afghanistan, satellite recon
and smart bombs cannot replace soldiers
on the ground. When a SEAL team SeaHawk
helicopter goes down in the icy mountains of
Kandahar, Lieutenant Lester Donovan must
make a difficult decision — follow orders or go
"off mission" and save his fellow soldiers. With
Taliban terrorists at every turn, neither decision
will be easy. He'll need his instincts and some
high-tech weaponry to get off of the hillside
and back to base alive!

Art Director: Bob Lentz
Graphic Designer: Brann Garvey
Production Specialist: Michelle Biedscheid

Photo credits: DoD photo by Spc. Michael J.
MacLeod, U.S. Army, 44; Getty Images Inc.:
AFP, 7,
Robert Nickelsberg, 21, Spencer Platt, 20, Time
Life Pictures/Mai/Mai/Greg Mathieson, 33;
Shutterstock: CreativeHQ, 64, RCPPHOTO, 33;
U.S. Marine Corps photo by Cpl. Christopher R.
Rye, 45; U.S. Navy Photo, 21, 81, MC3 Nicholas
Hall, 32, MCC Jeremy L. Wood, 65, PH1 Tim
Turner, 80

Printed in the United States of America
in Stevens Point, Wisconsin
092010   005934WZS11

TABLE OF CONTENTS

PERSONNEL FILE

Lieutenant Commander
LESTER DONOVAN

ORGANIZATION:
U.S. Navy SEALs

ENTERED SERVICE AT:
Naval Amphibious Base Coronado in
San Diego, CA

BORN:
April 15, 1972

EQUIPMENT

Protective Goggles

Bulletproof Vest

M4 Carbine

Ammo Belt

M1911 Pistol

First-Aid Pouch

Karambit Knife

Combat Boots

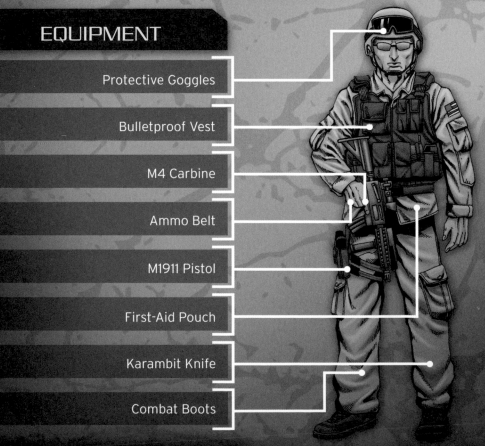

OVERVIEW: AFGHANISTAN

On September 11, 2001, the terrorist group Al-Qaeda attacked the United States, hijacking four commercial airliners and flying three of them into buildings along the East Coast. President George W. Bush and the U.S. military responded quickly. On October 7, 2001, they began Operation Enduring Freedom, attempting to shut down Al-Qaeda hideouts in Afghanistan and capture their leader, Osama Bin Laden. In recent years, the military campaign has evolved into a counter-insurgency operation – tactics to keep the Afghan government and citizens in favor of U.S. policy.

Osama Bin Laden

MAP

AFGHANISTAN

Kandahar

MISSION

When a SEAL team Seahawk helicopter goes down in the icy mountains of Kandahar, Lieutenant Commander Lester Donovan must make a difficult decision – follow orders or go "off mission" and save his fellow soldiers.

CHAPTER 001

SNATCH AND GRAB

The temperature of the wind that blew over the SEAL's face amazed him. Most times, one welcomes a breeze on a summer day, but not here. Not in this place.

Afghanistan was an entirely different beast, and there was never any cool air. It was hot, like a blow-dryer. The granules of sand that swirled in the breeze made the wind even more unwelcome. The SEAL squinted, doing his best not to get sand in his eyes. But even though sand kept pounding at his face through the open door of the flying SH-60 Seahawk, he was a very happy man.

Today saw mission accomplishment for Lieutenant Commander Lester Donovan, Team Leader of 2nd Platoon, SEAL Team Two. It was an especially sweet victory because it was Donovan's first outing as their commanding officer. The Team had always respected Donovan's leadership, but a couple of older sailors had initially questioned his promotion.

To them, Donovan seemed like a by-the-book officer. He wouldn't bend on situations the master chiefs knew they might encounter down range. They wanted a commanding officer who could adapt and be as flexible as the situation demanded.

Donovan understood this type of sidestepping. He didn't like that some sailors felt they were above the law. He knocked the Team back pretty hard sometimes, but they respected him for it. For that reason, and because he was, hands-down, the best shot in Team Two. He could pick fleas off a dog from 100 yards with just the iron sights of his gun. And he knew this impressed the men, especially the older guys, even if they never showed it.

This mission was about as textbook as a SEAL operation could get, and it had gone off without a hitch. It was a standard snatch and grab. They had been tasked with the capture of Taliban leader Majad Raman Hassan. And they had gotten him without one casualty. The sixteen men of 2nd Platoon were all coming home alive and well. Eight of the SEALs rode in the first bird. The second eight occupied another Seahawk helicopter not far off their starboard side.

Seaman Second Class Williams, the team's sniper, chuckled as he looked out the helicopter door. He closed his eyes and let the wind whip his face.

"This is just like back home!" the big southerner said as he basked in the heat.

One of the other SEALs, Petty Officer Kaili, the team's corpsman, just snarled. "Of course you love this, you BBQ-eating, Texas-Longhorn hillbilly! Man, all you Southern dudes just dig the heat! Me?" Kaili made a wave-like motion with his hand. "I'm a water man, myself!"

"That's cause you was born on an island in the Pacific, brah!" Williams laughed and hula danced with his hands. "Where's your grass skirt, Hawaiian-boy?"

"At your mom's house, *haole*!" Kaili laughed.

The old man of 3rd Platoon, Master Chief Petty Officer Miller, just smirked and shook his head.

"There he goes, droppin' the mom bomb again," Miller said. "Kaili, when are you gonna come up with something new?"

But Kaili smiled and shot back, "As soon as you can start keeping up!"

"Ohhhhhh!" the men all shouted and laughed.

Donovan was proud to be a part of this team. They were a tight-knit band of brothers. They made fun of each other, tossed around macho jokes, and played all day long. But they trusted each other with their lives. Behaving like a family strengthened that brotherly bond, but when it came time to do their jobs, playtime was over. They became locked-on, like laser sights, and were the best at what they did.

Team Two were known in the Special Ops community for being experts at cold weather warfare. They trained for months in Anchorage, Alaska under harsh conditions. They were snow masters. They could go anywhere it was cold and beat the enemy at their own game. Team Two was ready for the winters in Afghanistan.

In a post-9/11 world, U.S. President George W. Bush decided the best defense against terrorism was a strong offense. He ordered troops into Afghanistan to attack the Taliban where they slept.

That decision meant fighting in caves deep in the snow-covered mountains of Kandahar.

As seasons changed, the SEALs of Team Two traded in their parkas for moisture-wicking tactical t-shirts and went hunting for a second tour. Hunting in the super-hot temperatures and sand-swirling winds.

After a devastating ambush weeks earlier, many members of the Team had made the ultimate sacrifice and new leadership was sought.

Enter Donovan.

Having proven himself an invaluable Team member, Donovan was given an unwanted battlefield promotion. His Team Leader had been killed in action entering a warehouse to evict local terrorists who were hiding there. Only through fast actions and motivating leadership did Donovan help his SEALs bring a relatively positive close to an otherwise messy situation. Back at headquarters, he found himself promoted to the lead position — though he never wanted it.

Especially not because his Team Leader had died.

The Seahawk helicopters dipped, floated across the sands, and passed over farmhouses. The prisoner in Donovan's chopper looked out the main hatch as the farming village slid by underneath them. He frowned as he looked at the ground and started mumbling.

Kaili bent forward and whispered in the terrorist's ear. "Pray all you want. Ain't gonna help you, brah," he said.

The man turned and glared at Kaili for a moment. Then he continued praying quietly.

Looking starboard, Donovan saw the other half of his team riding in the other Seahawk. He grinned as he placed a hand up to his ear and yelled into his microphone.

"Alpha Three, Team Leader, over?" he said.

In the other chopper, a young lieutenant, Mike Barnett from Huntsville, Alabama, looked across the gulf of hot air at his commanding officer. He smiled.

"What can I do for you, sir?" Barnett asked.

"How's everyone doing, over?" replied Donovan.

"Riding high on the —" Barnett began.

KABLAMO!

There was a flash of sparkling light and a brilliant blast of heat. Donovan watched in horror as the nearby chopper was instantly turned into a burning mass of twisted and crumpled metal.

A glance at the ground told the story. A team of three men stood on a berm on the far end of one of the farms. They were reloading rocket-propelled grenade launchers with fresh ammo.

The Seahawk had been shot out of the skies by a Taliban RPG team.

Reacting quickly, Donovan turned to the cockpit, yelling into his microphone.

"RPG! RP —" he shouted.

He was cut off in mid-sentence as the tail rotor of his aircraft exploded and detached. It splintered into a million metal shavings that littered the skies.

The chopper spun wildly. It twisted in the opposite direction of the rotors as it fell out of the sky.

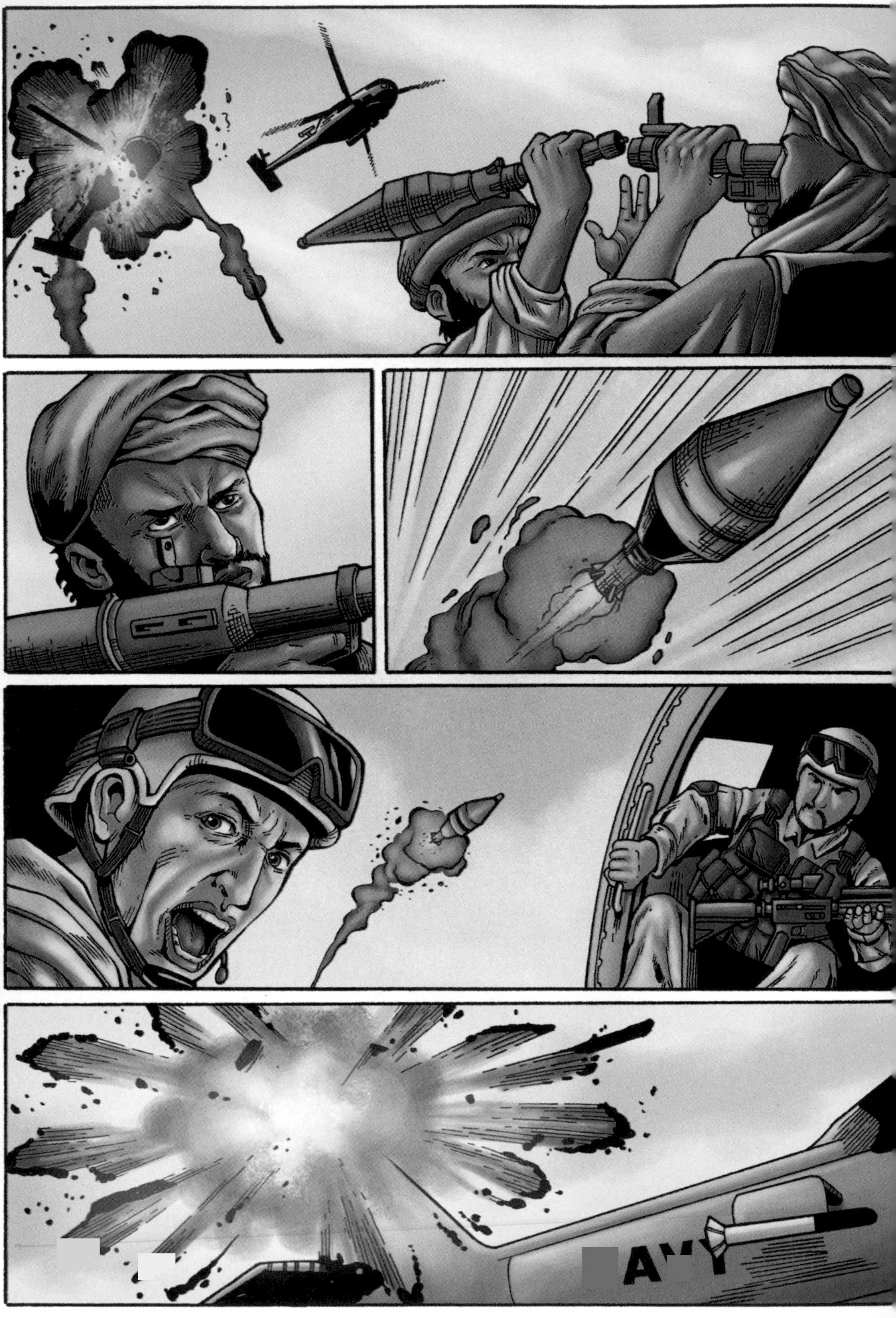

The ground rushed up quickly. The pilot did his best to rotate and slow the chopper's descent, but it didn't seem to help.

In a matter of seconds, the chopper slammed into the sand and burst into flames.

Inside, the men were shaken and rattled. The explosion had cracked through the cabin, killing four of the sailors and knocking the master chief unconscious.

The pilot had done his best to save his passengers and crew. But the chopper's control panel had caved into him and his co-pilot, killing them both.

Donovan had been knocked against the main cabin bulkhead during the crash. He was dizzy and immobile. He saw nothing but the white haze of smoke, the orange glow of flames, and his men dying.

A concussion was the least of his problems. He was vaguely aware of five robed men, obviously locals, reaching into the inferno. They pulled his high-valued target from the rubble.

Majad Raman Hassan had been liberated.

A low, steady hum and a high-pitched ringing filled Donovan's ears. Unable to focus, and seeing three of everything, the lieutenant commander tried to reach for his weapon, but he couldn't find it. It had come out of his holster and been tossed across the wreckage.

The Taliban took everything that wasn't nailed down. Equipment bags, weapons, ammo, explosives.

And worst of all . . . they took the survivors.

Majad Raman Hassan was now free to give orders again. The terrorist pointed at Williams and Kaili, both still alive. The men were dazed, but they tried their best to fight back. For their efforts, the aggressors beat them senseless.

Donovan tried to move, struggled to help, but there was nothing he could do. His safety harness wouldn't budge. Blackness rapidly washed over him like oil seeping into the water.

And all of a sudden, his world was dark.

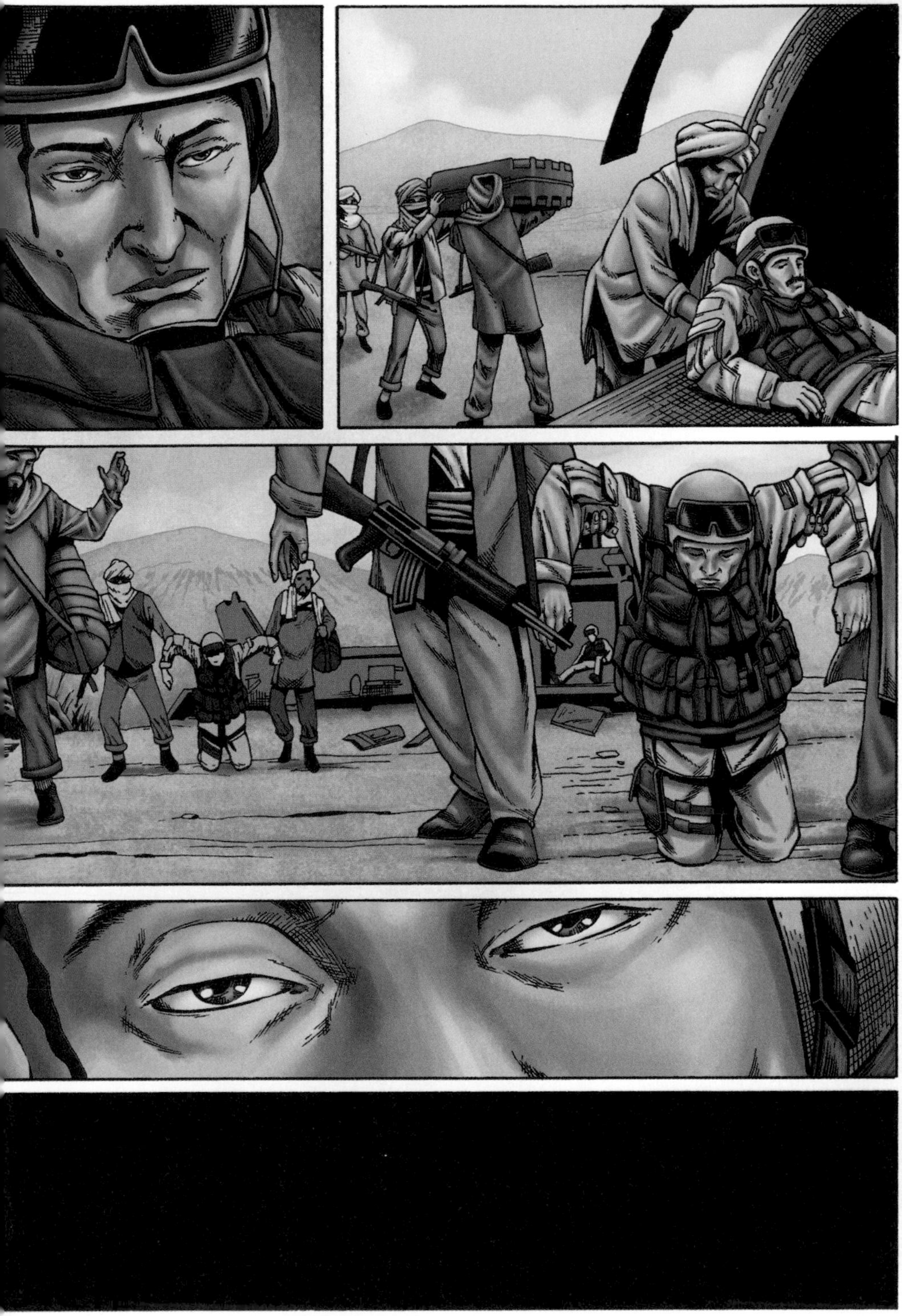

DEBRIEFING

SEPTEMBER 11, 2001

HISTORY

On the morning of September 11, 2001, the terrorist group Al-Qaeda hijacked four commercial airliners. The events of that day began the War on Terror and forever changed the United States:

8:45 a.m. – American Airlines Flight 11 crashes into the north tower of the World Trade Center (WTC) in New York.

9:03 a.m. – United Airlines Flight 175 crashes into the south tower of the WTC.

9:30 a.m. – President informs public of a "terrorist attack."

9:40 a.m. – American Airlines Flight 77 hits the Pentagon.

10:05 a.m. – The south tower of the WTC collapses.

10:10 a.m. – United Airlines Flight 93 crashes into a field southeast of Pittsburgh.

10:28 a.m. – The north tower of the WTC collapses.

During these events, nearly 3,000 people lost their lives, including hundreds of police, fire fighters, and other rescue workers responding to the attacks.

THE TALIBAN

HISTORY

The political and religious group known as the Taliban took power in Afghanistan in 1996. During their reign, this militant group forced the citizens of their country to follow strict religious rules. Women were treated poorly, banned from working, and not allowed to attend schools. Minorities and followers of other religions were forced to leave the country or be killed. In 2001, Osama bin Laden took refuge in Afghanistan. When the Taliban refused to turn him over to the United States, the U.S. military attacked and eventually overthrew the organization.

RPGS

RPGs, or Rocket-Propelled Grenades, are a weapon of choice for Taliban soldiers.

CHAPTER 002

TIES THAT BIND

Licking at his hands, the cabin flames woke Donovan from unconsciousness. As he looked around, dazed, he'd almost forgotten his situation. Then the sight of the charred remains of his teammates lying across the wreckage snapped him back to reality.

A slight moaning, coming from under the layers of warped sheet metal, made him turn. "Master Chief!" he yelled, reaching for the pieces of steel pinning Miller to the ground.

Donovan dealt with his pain as he pried away the hot sheet metal, but it was slow going. Outside, the fire moved dangerously close to the spent fuel flowing from the tanks. The flames grew hotter and hotter. Donovan knew they only had a few moments before the entire chopper went up like a Roman candle.

Struggling, Donovan could feel the metal budge. Miller looked up at his chief officer. They both knew there wasn't any more time.

"GO! Get the heck outta here, sir!" Miller grumbled as Donovan strained to lift the heavy metal.

The flames inched closer to the fuel stream.

"Sir, please! Leave me, just — just go!" cried Miller.

The metal began to move. Donovan was able to jam his shoulder under the plate. Now he could use his legs for leverage.

As the metal shifted, Miller scooted from under the heavy materials.

FWOOOSH!

The flame finally touched the leaking fuel. Once the fuel ignited, a burning stream of fire started barreling toward the chopper at an uncontrollably fast rate.

Donovan quickly helped Miller to his feet. As they stumbled from the helicopter, Donovan grabbed the only remaining piece of equipment that hadn't been stolen or destroyed — a canvas weapons bag. The SEALs bolted from the crash as the fire finally reached the fuel tanks.

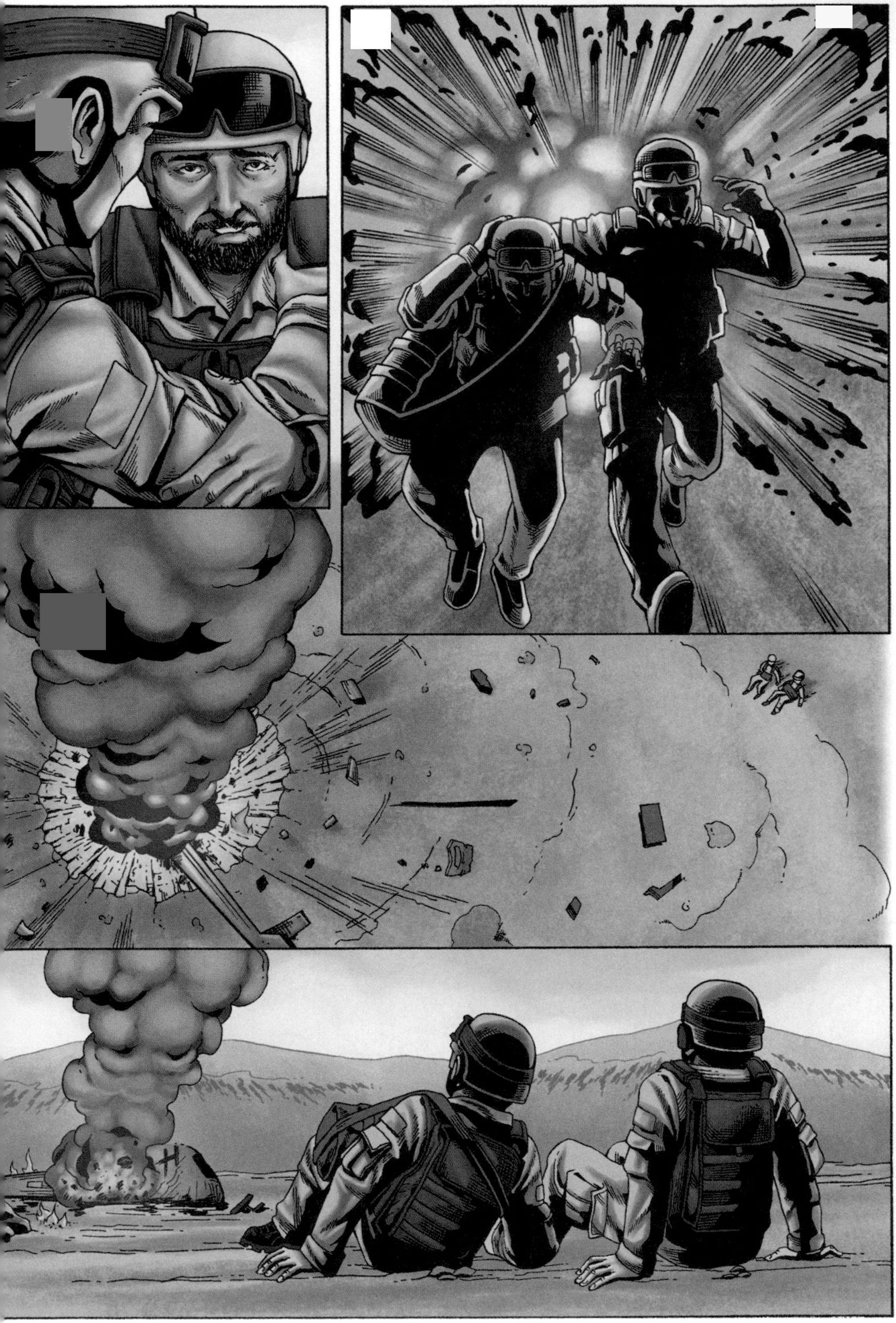

The enormous eruption created a shock wave that rippled through the air and slammed into both men. They tumbled and rolled to the ground as flaming debris sailed past them.

They lay on their backs, breathing heavily. Looking at Donovan, Miller smiled. "Glad you did all those boot camp exercises now, sir?" he said with a laugh.

Donovan groaned and grabbed at his back. "I know *you* are! Who knew all those squats would save your life?" he replied.

Miller grinned as he opened the canvas bag. He pulled an M4 carbine out of the canvas container and snapped a suppressor on it. "It's Williams's gear bag," said Miller. "We've got two M4s with silencers, two MK23s, and a butt-load of ammo for both. Some other goodies in here, too, but I'd say it's just what we need to rescue our —"

Donovan cut him off. "No."

The thirty-seven-year-old master chief turned to the younger lieutenant commander. Donovan began loading his M4 with a fresh magazine of ammo.

"What do you mean, 'No'?" Miller asked, shocked.

"Exactly that," answered Donovan. "Our first priority is to get outta here and report what happened."

"No way, sir!" Miller stood, ratcheting the charging handle of the weapon. "We need to jump out there and get our boys back from —"

"From who?!" Donovan yelled. "Huh? When you were face down in the wreckage, did you see who took them? Where they took them? Or even which way they went?"

"No, but —" Miller began.

"But what, Master Chief?" Donovan asked. "We don't even have a starting point. No communications, limited supplies, and no idea of where we are." He took the second M4 from the bag and loaded it.

After slinging the bag over his shoulder, Donovan stuck the butt of his rifle into the sand and held it still. Since he knew their location on the globe and the time of day, Donovan could get a compass bearing based on the way the shadow of his weapon fell on the sand.

Donovan looked at his watch.

A small sense of sadness fell over the lieutenant commander. Cracked and splintered, the glass lens of the watch's face was barely holding on.

The old Bernus WWII watch was an heirloom. It had been passed down from generation to generation of military men in his family. When he signed up for Officer Candidate School, Donovan's father had given it to him. This had been his great uncle's watch. He'd worn it during his jump into Normandy in WWII. When he came home, he'd given it to his brother, Lester's grandfather, before Korea. It had then passed from Lester's grandfather to his dad when Verner was shipped off to Vietnam.

The watch meant a lot to the family. Lester often heard stories of its travels across the globe. But when his father had given it to him, Lester had been floored. His father had told him, "If you're going to be part of the service, then by God, you're going in as a Donovan!"

Service hadn't been his father's wish for Lester. He'd wanted Lester to follow his dreams, to become a journalist, to report on the world, not to be a part of its bloodshed. Their family had given enough to the country.

But after the attacks of September 11, Lester Donovan knew he couldn't stand by and let other people take risks protecting his personal freedoms while he reported on it. He wanted to be part of something bigger than himself. He wanted to be on the front lines of a war that needed people like him — natural leaders.

His father and grandfather were proud of Lester when he got his golden "Budweiser" Trident of the Navy SEALs at graduation. After the helicopter attack, and the loss of their Taliban prisoner, Lester wondered if they would be proud of him now.

But the watch kept ticking, even though it had been smashed, and that made Donovan smile. If the watch could keep working, he could, too. The falling shadow from the weapon, plus the time from his watch, soon gave him a compass heading.

"We go that way," he said, pointing. "The Hindu Kush mountains."

Miller's eyes narrowed. It was going to be a rough hump, but they could do it. Water was all they needed and hopefully, they could find it along their route.

Miller looked over to Donovan. "Look, sir," he said. "I know what the book says, but I really think we need to find our men."

"This was planned," said Donovan. "They knew our route, and they shot us out of the skies. I know you think I'm new and I don't care, but you're wrong. If I knew where they were, if I had any clue, we'd go in there back-to-back like Rambo and Marcinko. But I don't, and neither do you. Their tracks were cleared away by the wind, and all I know is that the base is north from here." Donovan adjusted his bag. "We've got a long hump, so let's get moving. I'll take the lead."

With those words, the conversation was over. They were heading back to base and that was final.

Donovan could tell that Miller wasn't happy, but he believed there wasn't any other option.

Somehow, the Taliban figured out the path of the choppers, and that was important information. They were one of three Teams sent out to capture targets in the area. This couldn't happen to the other ones. Miller and Donovan had to get this info back to base soon.

The sun was sinking on the horizon, and Donovan knew it would cool off soon. Even a nightfall of 85 degrees was better than high noon in the desert.

Sand kicked away from their Special Forces' boots as they slowly, cautiously trekked toward the mountains.

SH-60 SEAHAWK

SPECIFICATIONS

FIRST FLIGHT: 12-12-1979
ROTOR: 53 feet 8 inches
LENGTH: 64 feet 8 inches
HEIGHT: 17 feet 2 inches
WEIGHT: 15,200 pounds
MAX SPEED: 207 mph
CRUISE SPEED: 168 mph
CEILING: 12,000 feet
CREW: Two (pilot and electronic warfare officer)

FACT

Seahawks deploy "sonobuoys," which, when dropped into the ocean, relay the location of enemy submarines.

HISTORY

The U.S. Navy replaced older, often heavier, helicopters with SH-60 Seahawks during the 1970s. Twin turboshaft engine and deployment possibilities make Seahawks popular aircraft for surface warfare, anti-submarine warfare, and search and rescue missions. The typical SH-60 Seahawk carries a crew of three to four people and can deploy from and land on nearly any surface, including destroyers, cruisers, or assault ships. Each Seahawk helicopter also carries several torpedoes, missiles, and a machine gun.

M4 Carbine

HISTORY

TYPE: Carbine
SERVICE: 1997–present
WEIGHT: 5.9 pounds
LENGTH: 33 inches
BARREL: 14.5 inches
HISTORY: Since the late 1990s, the M4 carbine has played a major role in U.S. military conflicts, such as the war in Iraq and the war in Afghanistan. This gas-powered, magazine-fed weapon is shorter and lighter than a full-length rifle, making it ideal for urban-combat situations. Able to fire up to 950 rounds per minute, the M4 can provide quick cover-fire and protect troops on the ground.

MK23 PISTOL

For closer range, U.S. special operations forces rely on the MK23 semi-automatic pistol.

CHAPTER 003

COMMAND
AND CONQUER

Within hours, their plans had changed. The mountain ridge was shorter than they'd expected. Miller and Donovan explored the area and soon came upon a hideout. Most strongholds of this type were usually just holes in the side of a mountain that looked like they were made by gophers. But not this one. This one was well hidden by large outcroppings of rock and natural stone formations that surrounded the mouth of the stronghold.

It's like the entrance to the Batcave, Donovan thought. *No wonder we missed this one.*

The ridgeline didn't allow them as much cover as he would have liked. But it didn't matter to Donovan who lay in the dirt, looking into the mouth of the cave about two hundred yards ahead. They were going to have to go in the front door either way. This was just another challenge.

To the left, a small generator sat, chugging away and belching black clouds of smoke into the air.

The lines from the old generator ran into the mouth of the cave, obviously feeding the area with electricity. To the SEALs, it was a yellow brick road, leading to the place where the Taliban were probably keeping their soldiers.

The two Americans quietly used their hands to move the sand and dirt from underneath them. They dug in for the long haul. They needed to observe the area, making sure they learned all they could about the men inside. If that meant sitting still and watching, no matter how long it took, then that's what they would do.

Donovan rummaged in the equipment bag. A huge smile crossed his face as he pulled out a foot-long, remote-controlled airplane body.

"No way . . ." Miller said with a smirk. "That's gonna make life a whole lot easier."

The RQ-11A Raven UAV was ready for flight. After switching on the remote, Donovan had the infrared camera send data to the handheld video device.

Donovan clicked on the silent motor, and rising up slightly, threw the small plane into the air. The drone flew off without a sound and swept into the night.

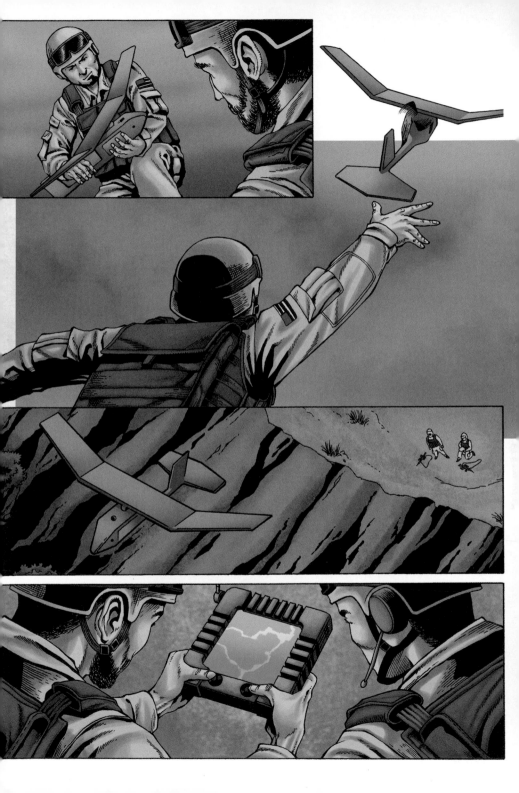

Both men took shifts flying the drone and reviewing the data it was transmitting back. Several hours passed before either of them had anything to report.

Soon, however, they located the same five robed men from the attack. Out front, two guards on a roving patrol were relieved every two hours. Of the men that had made the switch, only one had repeated, so it was safe to assume they were correct in their counting.

The Taliban men were armed with rifles, but that seemed to be all. No explosives. No grenades. Their lack of weaponry would make things easier on the two SEALs.

"Okay," Donovan began as the Raven came back and landed next to them. "Here's the plan."

Donovan was to sneak toward the main entrance while Miller waited, perched in an over-watch position with his weapon, covering his movements.

When Donovan was close enough to the front entrance, he would take out the left guard at the main entrance nearest to the generator. Then the master chief would snipe the other from his position.

At that point, Miller would join Donovan. They would cut the power to the generator, causing a blackout inside the cave. Hopefully, the Taliban fighters would assume that the generator was malfunctioning for some reason, forcing one of the other guards to the entrance. Then he would be hit, leaving only two to watch their prisoners inside.

Donovan was sure that they would find the place where the SEALs were being held. With reasonable losses to the enemy, they'd get their friends out easily, thanks to their night-vision goggles.

Miller laughed. "Reasonable?" he asked.

"I don't want a bloodbath," answered Donovan. "But if someone gets in your way, put 'em down because we're going home. With everyone."

"Including Hassan?" asked Miller, pulling a high-powered scope from his equipment bag. He locked it onto the top of his M4 carbine.

Nodding, Donovan answered, "If he's in there, he's going back."

"Hooyah, sir," Miller responded.

Donovan reached down and grabbed a handful of
dirt. He spat on it, and rubbed it on his face. He looked
over to Miller.

"How do I look?" he asked.

Miller shook his head and smiled. "Like you should be
eatin' worms," he replied.

Miller crawled to the left. Donovan made his way
around to the generator and the cave entrance.

Crawling to the left flank of the generator took Donovan twenty minutes. When he finally got there, the changing of the guards was taking place.

Donovan waited patiently and quietly. The replacement guard pulled out a canteen of water and offered it to the other man.

Oh man, great, Donovan thought. *I'm going to be here all night!*

But to his surprise, the man didn't want the water. The first guard left, leaving the relief to drink by himself.

Five minutes later, Donovan began to move.

He slowly reached down and removed the karambit knife from the sheath tied to his left boot. He held the knife in his hand so that its blade curved forward from the bottom of his fist.

Then Donovan positioned himself on the balls of his feet. He suddenly sprang forward. He covered his prey's mouth with his left hand. The guard fell instantly behind the generator, and Donovan finished him.

As he'd expected, when the first guard went down, the second guard on the right turned. He raised his weapon to fire.

BANG! BANG!

The enemy's chest jerked twice as shots entered his torso. He dropped to the deck. Miller's aim was spot-on. Quickly, Miller joined Donovan at the mouth of the cave.

"Noise discipline," Donovan said. "Hand signals!"

Donovan's night-vision goggles flipped down over his right eye and powered on. The blackness of night lit up in green and white hues.

With a thumbs-up from Miller, they stepped inside.

RQ-11A RAVEN UAV

SPECIFICATIONS

TYPE: SUAV (Small Unmanned
Aerial Vehicle)
FIRST FLIGHT: 10-2001
LENGTH: 36 inches
WEIGHT: 4.2 pounds
WING SPAN: 55 inches
RANGE: 6.2 miles
CEILING: 1,000 feet
CREW: 0

FACT

A single RQ-11 Raven system costs
$250,000, but the unmanned
vehicles provide priceless
information for modern soldiers.

HISTORY

In modern warfare, unmanned
aerial vehicles (UAVs) are essential
devices for aerial surveillance and
precision bombing. Introduced in
2003, the RQ-11A Raven also had
the advantage of its small size.
At a little more than four pounds,
soldiers can hand-launch the RQ-11
Raven from nearly any location.
After the UAV has been deployed,
troops can control the vehicle
by remote or program its flight
path into a high-tech GPS (Global
Positioning System). While in
flight, the RQ-11 Raven sends back
aerial photographs to troops on
the ground.

NIGHT-VISION DEVICES (NVDs)

HISTORY

As early as World War II, militaries have used night-vision devices (NVDs) in battle. However, first generation NVDs had limited capabilities. They could view objects at no more than a few hundred feet away, and were too heavy to transport. During the Vietnam War, the technology advanced, and some soldiers carried rifles with night vision telescopic sights, called Starlight scopes. Today, U.S. soldiers often wear small, helmet-mounted night vision goggles in darkened combat situations, such as fighting the hillside caves of Afghanistan.

MODERN WAR

UAVs and NVDs are only a small fraction of the new technologies used during in modern wars like the war in Afghanistan. Lightweight body armor, drone bombers, and specialized tanks allow U.S. troops to be safe and effective soldiers. Even today, however, standard-issue helmets, rifles, and boots, much like those used in WWII, continue to be the most important protection for soldiers on the battlefield.

CHAPTER 004

INTO THE LION'S DEN

Weapons held high, their butt stocks pressed tightly to their shoulders, the men walked in step — Miller on the left, Donovan on the right. With every third step, they swept the weapons and made sure there was no one behind them.

The darkness glowed in hues of green as they explored the cave as silently as possible. Although they were taking it slow, their combat boots on a rocky and sandy surface still made noise.

A gradual slope of about fifty yards led downward into the mountain. The cave began to widen. Partially hand-carved, but mostly natural, the stone was smooth to the touch and damp. Donovan had always found this fact odd. He thought stone in the desert would be dry, but it seemed some of these caves were like sponges, sweating in the darkness.

The wires from the generator were their road map. Miller and Donovan followed them, fastened to the ceiling, deeper down into the darkness.

Suddenly, the beam from a flashlight and the sound of footsteps approached. Both men stopped. They flattened themselves against the wall in the darkness as Taliban soldiers came toward them.

One of the guards had been dispatched to see what was wrong with the generator. Unfortunately for him, Miller was waiting. Placing a hand over the enemy's mouth, the SEAL maneuvered a knife to the man's throat and pulled him in tightly.

Donovan retrieved the fallen flashlight and shined it in the guard's face, blinding him. He questioned the man in Pashto. "Where are they keeping the Americans?" he asked softly.

Eyes closed tightly and his face full of fear, the man nodded and pointed. Miller removed his knife just long enough for the man to tell them the SEALs were down a passageway about 100 meters, then in the cavern to the right.

Donovan turned off the flashlight, and Miller finished the job. As the terrorist's body crumpled to the floor, the men moved on.

Finally, the SEALs turned a corner and stopped in their tracks. This wasn't just a cave for five men. It was a massive subterranean network of caves that led into other parts of the countryside! There were dozens of passageways that branched off from here. Donovan and Miller had just traveled into the lion's den.

This was a central hub, a junction point, for all enemy operations in this part of the country. Three separate underground passageways led off in front of them to other parts of the desert. As far as they could see, those three passageways had several different branches that opened up further down into their own system of maze-like tunnels. One tunnel on their left led into what looked like a small storage room. The one to the right was where they assumed their U.S. comrades were held.

Usually, these types of caves were just dead ends, with only enough room for a cot and a lantern. Not this one. This was more like a subway system for terrorists.

Donovan had heard rumors of this place but had never believed them. Seeing it, he was speechless.

"They . . . they must have been working on this for years," Miller whispered, breaking the silence.

Nodding, Donovan looked to the front-right passage, where two other men appeared with flashlights. The Taliban soldiers were heading right at them. If the SEALs didn't move, they'd surely be discovered.

Moving left, they ducked into the small storage room. Donovan and Miller flattened themselves against the walls as the two men passed by.

Donovan bumped something. He turned to see several wooden crates piled high against the walls. Tapping Miller on the shoulder, he thumbed at the boxes.

"A weapons cache," whispered Miller.

Several crates of AK-47s and RPGs sat ready to be used against other NATO soldiers. The weapons that had shot down their chopper had come from here. This fact was obvious because, more importantly, his team's stolen gear sat on a table behind the boxes.

Donovan picked up ammo, pistols, night-vision goggles, and even plastic explosives. He placed it all into a canvas bag and tossed it over to Miller. The master chief slung it across his back.

"For the boys," Miller said.

Donovan nodded, looking around for more goodies.

"Yeah, and let's leave these guys with a bang. Sound good?" Miller asked.

Donovan agreed and motioned for Miller to wire up the crates with the explosives. Miller took a small brick of Composite Four out of the equipment bag. He began to mash it up and spread it along the edges of the crates like a thick line of toothpaste.

As he searched around for whatever else he could find, Donovan looked toward the end of the small room. He suddenly stopped and smiled.

On the end of the small table, sat an old-style Vietnam-era radio. He lifted the handset, turned a few of the frequency dials, and was about to hit TRANSMIT, when something caught his eye.

A detailed topographical map lay on the table, marked up in red pen. Lines and shapes circled and connected U.S. troop locations and movements from all across the region. The enemy had done their homework. Through their own type of recon, the Taliban had learned deployment schedules and the U.S. timetables for patrols.

They've got everything on us, our entire mission They must have been watching us for months, a year even! Donovan thought. Instinctively, the lieutenant commander grabbed the map, folded it up, and shoved it into his pocket.

Donovan cautiously pressed TRANSMIT and whispered into the handset.

"Ghost Hunter Actual, this is Ghost Hunter Two, do you copy?" He released the transmit button.

Nothing. Just a low static. His heart sank. Maybe the battery was dying, maybe they were too far out of —

"Ghost Hunter Two, this is Actual, go ahead," suddenly crackled out of the handset.

A large smile crossed Donovan's face as he pulled a small, folded map from his right cargo pocket.

"Man, are we happy to hear you!" Donovan said. "Ghost Hunter One is gone. We are currently involved in CSAR operations and need emergency evac at these coordinates." He read off their location into the handset.

"Roger," said the radio operator. "We will have someone to you in thirty minutes."

"Also request a bunker buster air strike at this locale. We're sitting on a group of terrorists in underground tunnels. It's like Grand Central Station down here," Donovan said softly.

"Roger that," said the RO. "Air strike approved at those coordinates. I suggest you make haste."

"Like rabbits in mating season," Donovan said. "Out." He placed the handset on the table and moved over to Miller, who had just finished setting the explosive charges.

"Timer?" Miller asked.

"No — detonator. Here, you take it," said Donovan. "Might need it to cover our exit. We've got thirty minutes. If we can't do it in that time, we're all dead anyway."

"Okay," Miller replied. He pulled the magazine out of his weapon and slapped the back end of it against his leg. He made sure all the brass was packed neatly in the clip. After slapping it back in, he pulled back the charging handle and got ready to rock. "Let's do this."

Silently, they moved from the storeroom and crossed into the dark hall. Three Taliban with flashlights were standing there, complaining about the lack of power. One of them was on a radio, reporting to someone outside, who was trying to figure out where the guards were. Donovan listened to the conversation.

"I've got three tangos. Two men outside at the generator. Can't find the guard," Donovan translated for Miller.

"We've got five minutes max then," Miller replied. "Say when." The master chief raised his weapon and took aim. Donovan did the same.

"Take 'em!" Donovan shouted.

All the men heard were whooshes of air as the silenced shots flew from the barrels of their M4s. Like sacks of wet potatoes, the three terrorists hit the ground, their flashlights clacking on the hard stone floor.

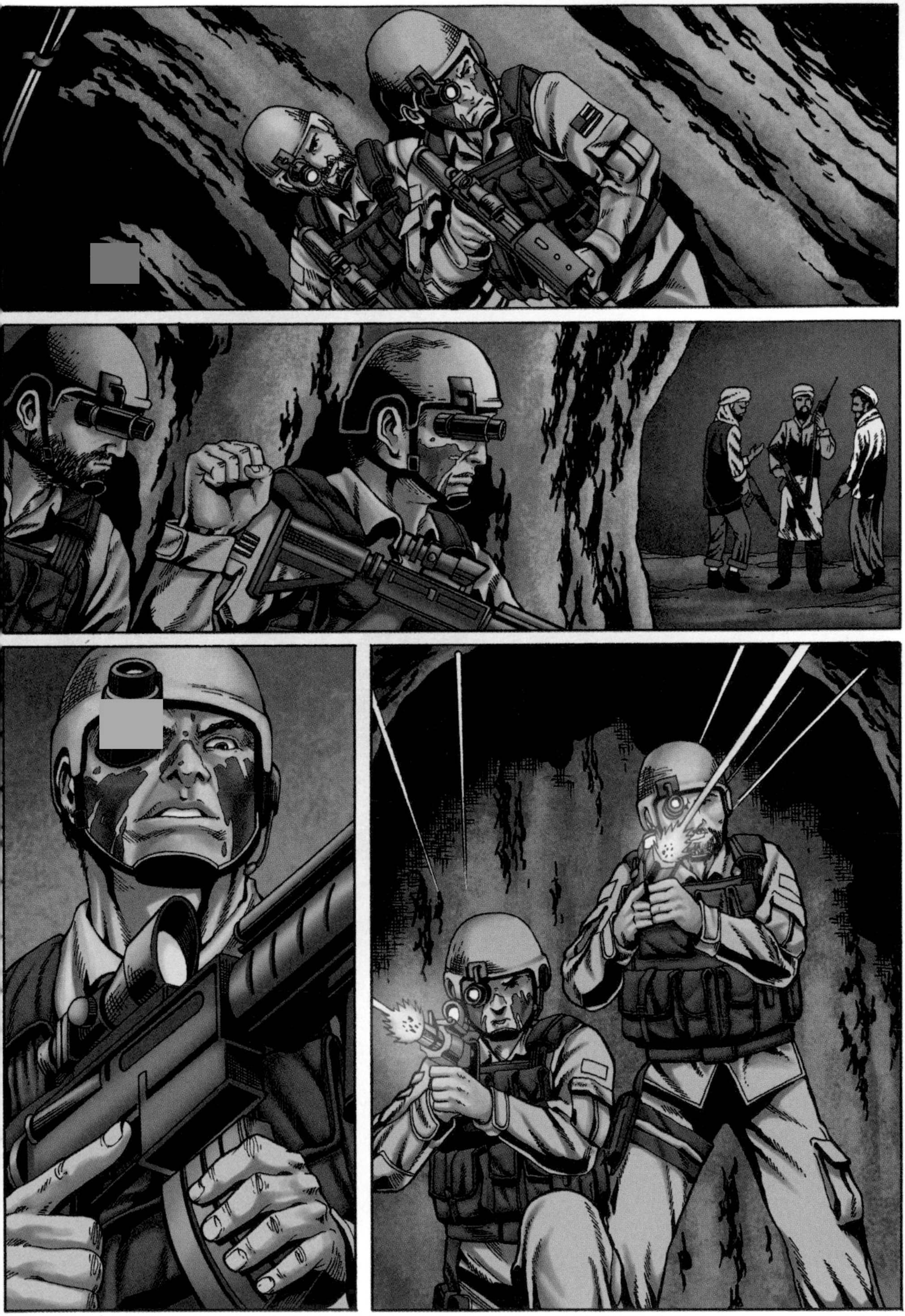

In a nearby room, Williams and Kaili, badly beaten, knelt on the dirt floor of the darkened cave. Their hands were tied behind their backs by hemp ropes.

Behind them, two large guards, both holding hacksaws stood quietly. They were ready to perform their sworn duty to execute the prisoners in the most horrific manner. A metal tripod topped by a small HD video camera waited to capture every frightful moment of the execution.

"Cursed lights!" the Taliban leader yelled. "You think we would have replaced that generator by now!"

From behind him, the fourth man in the room laughed. "Not to worry, Rojan," he said. "We will be rid of the infidels soon enough. It's probably just out of gas again."

Hassan entered, a piece of paper in his hands.

"It's nice to have you back, brother," the cameraman said as he slapped Hassan on the back. "How's the speech coming?"

On the ground, the two prisoners wheezed. Their raspy breathing echoed out into the small chamber. Both men were in bad shape, having been tortured and beaten for some time. Kaili, the Team's corpsman, looked over at Williams.

Blood flowed from his teammate's left ear. Bruises under his eyes had turned deep purple. His face was blue, his breathing getting harder and harder to push out with each passing minute.

"You hangin' in, brotha?" Kaili whispered softly so no one else could hear.

Williams nodded. "Sure. Probably just my allergies," he said with a grin.

"Keep the faith, they'll come for us . . ." Kaili said quietly.

Suddenly, a boot came down on the back of his neck, pinning him to the ground.

"No talking!" said Hassan from behind as he lifted his foot off of Kaili's neck. Reaching down, he grabbed Kaili by the hair and pulled him close, whispering in his ear.

"You'll have plenty of time to talk where you're going, brah," the Taliban leader joked. He slammed Kaili's head into the stone floor.

Kaili turned and glared at Hassan with a look that could melt marble. If he could get free, he'd show that guy a thing or two.

"DOWN!" a voice suddenly echoed into the room from nowhere.

Without hesitation, Kaili, who knew that man's voice better than his own, dove left. He shoved Williams to the ground as strategically placed M4 rounds flew through the air.

The first to fall was the left guard. The 5.6-mm NATO round blew through his chest and exited into the wall behind him.

The second guard made a move for his AK-47, but two perfectly placed lead projectiles walked up his arm and into his pectoral muscle. They ricocheted inside his chest cavity and exited out the other side of his torso, killing him instantly.

Closest to Donovan, the cameraman struck out with a right hook, but Donovan blocked it with the barrel of his rifle. In one full sweep, he pushed the man's fist aside and rammed the silencer into his face, breaking the man's nose. Crumpling to the floor, the man was no longer a threat.

Majad Raman Hassan, on the other hand, was still alive. He spun on his heels and raised a pistol in the air. He aimed at the back of Donovan's head.

With the butt of his weapon swinging like a baseball bat, Miller cold-cocked Hassan in the skull. The leader lost the gun — and consciousness — as he fell to the ground, out cold.

Quickly, Donovan used his knife to cut his teammate's restraints. He looked at Williams, and could tell he was hurt badly.

"I'm guessing he called them a lot of names they didn't quite like," he said.

"More than you'll ever know," Kaili answered back with a grin.

"Can you walk?" Miller asked as he handed Williams and Kaili both MK23 pistols.

"I'll . . . I'll freakin' run out of here if I have to, boss," Williams wheezed back. He stood tall, but he was still obviously in pain.

"Good, 'cuz we have to go —!" Miller stopped short as the lights in the cavern flickered back on.

"And him?" Miller asked as he motioned to Hassan.

"All of us, Master Chief!" Donovan said.

With a disappointed sigh, Miller reached down, tied Hassan's hands together, and picked him up in a fireman's carry across his back. He balanced the unconscious man on his shoulders so Miller could still fire his weapon from the hip if he needed to.

They moved out, Kaili taking point and Williams and Miller in the middle. Donovan checked the rear.

They made their way out of the holding area and into the hallway. All was clear for the moment, but as they rounded the corner into the central passageway, the men froze.

And that's when it happened.

Men flooded out of the passages like roaches in
the light. The SEALs were immediately spotted and
outnumbered. Shots from AKs rang out in the cave as
fifteen Taliban terrorists took aim and did their best to
stop the escapees.

Donovan took a knee as he returned fire. Bullets
sprayed from his weapon.

ATATAT! RATATAT! RATA

Bullets chipped up all around them as they provided
covering fire for one another. In typical SEAL style, they
leapfrogged out of harm's way, as one after another, they
peeled off the firing line. Moving to the rear, each man
covered the other's movements.

The exit of the cave was about fifty yards away now
as the terrorists continued their push. Miller threw off his
night-vision goggles when daylight started breaking over
the mountains and spilling into the mouth of the cave.

One of the terrorists stepped into the entrance. Hassan fell to the ground as Miller, fast as a cougar, pulled his knife out. In a quick glint of reflective light, the man at the foot of the cave was no longer a problem.

"Reloading!" Donovan yelled. He dropped the ammo magazine and reached for a fresh one. Kaili and Williams took careful aim with their pistols. The noise in the cave from all the automatic weapons fire was deafening.

"Move out!" Donovan ordered.

As Kaili and Williams ran, Miller aimed outbound, securing the exit ahead of them.

"Faster, faster, faster!" Miller yelled. Kaili and Williams finally came jogging up the fifty-yard slope.

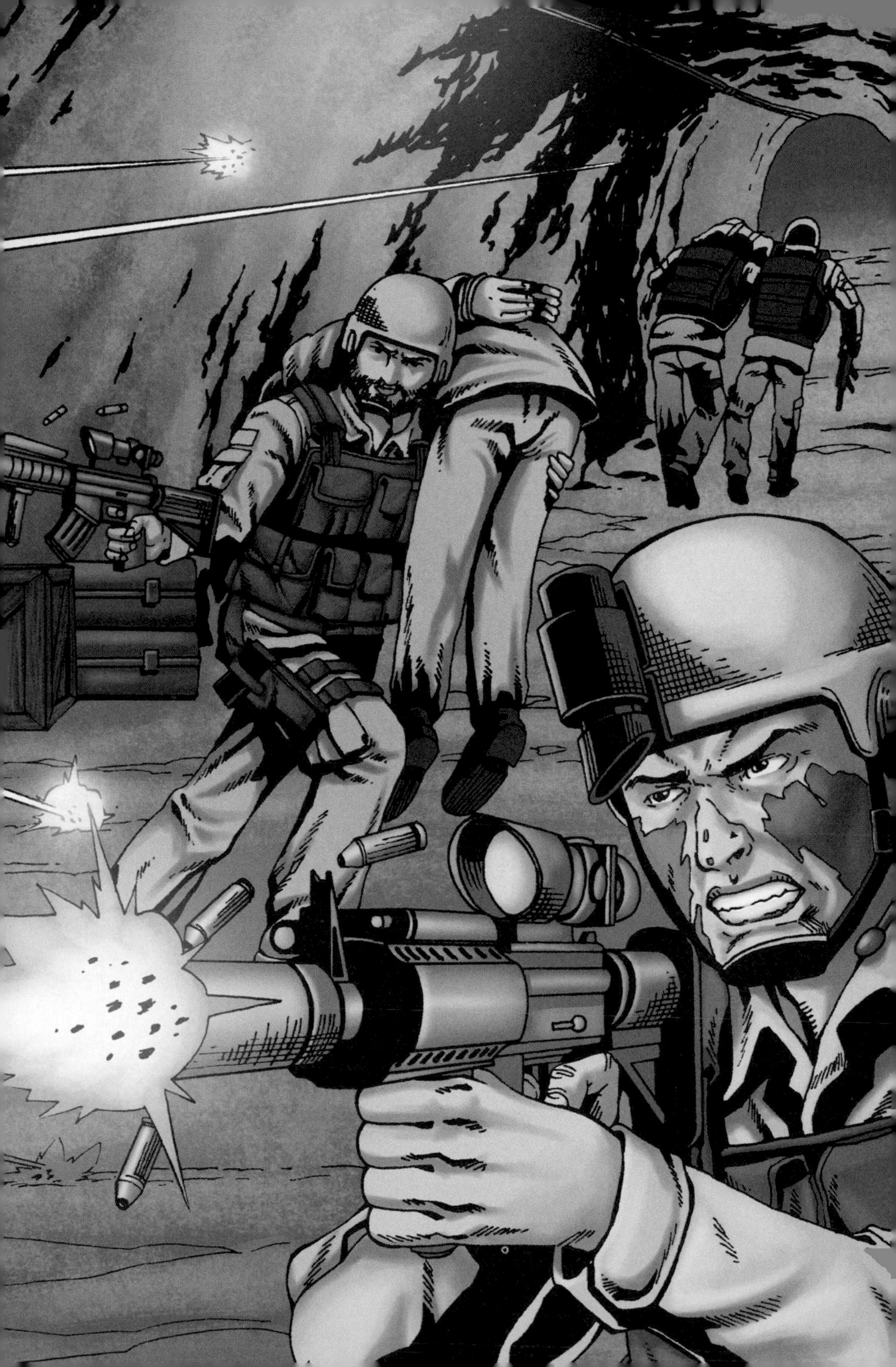

AK-47 ASSAULT RIFLE

SPECIFICATIONS

SERVICE: 1949-present
DESIGNER: Mikhail Kalashnikov
WEIGHT: 9.5 pounds
LENGTH: 34.3 inches with fixed
wooden stock; 34.4 inches with
folding stock extended; 25.4 inches
with stock folded
BARREL: 16.3 inches
RATE OF FIRE: 600 rounds/min.
EFFECTIVE RANGE: 330 yd, full-
automatic; 440 yd, semi-automatic

FACT

The AK-47 is also known as the
Kalash, a tribute to the designer.

HISTORY

The AK-47 was first developed in the
Soviet Union. It was one of the first
true assault rifles, and it continues
to be widely used today. It remains
popular because it has a low
production cost, is easy to use, and
is very durable. It can be fired as a
semi-automatic or full-automatic
rifle. In semi-automatic mode, it fires
only once when the trigger is pulled.
In full-automatic mode, the rifle
continues to fire until the rounds are
gone or until the trigger is released.
A versatile weapon, more AK-47s
have been produced than all other
assault weapons combined.

U.S. FORCES

HISTORY

On October 7, 2001, less than one month after the Al-Qaeda terrorist attacks on September 11, U.S. troops touched down in Afghanistan. Their mission: find Al-Qaeda leader Osama bin Laden and take out Taliban hideouts throughout the country. Other nations, including Great Britain, Germany, France, Italy, Spain, and Canada, joined in their efforts. By 2010, more than 90,000 U.S. soldiers were on the ground in Afghanistan. In ten years of fighting, nearly 1,400 U.S. soldiers had been lost on the battlefields.

IEDs

One of the biggest dangers for U.S. troops in Afghanistan are improvised explosive devices, or IEDs. Taliban soldiers place these homemade bombs along roadways and other high-traffic areas throughout the country. When military transports or even innocent civilians contact the IEDs, they explode. Difficult to detect, the U.S. military's best solution are "sniffer dogs." These hounds sniff out IEDs, allowing soldiers to safely dispose of the bombs.

CHAPTER 005
HOOYAH!

Weapon ready, Donovan crouched at the junction of the central chamber and the main slope. To his left was the weapons storeroom. In front of him, more Taliban members came flooding into the open hall.

He fired a few covering bursts as he got ready to move, but two more Taliban terrorists ran out from behind the cover of the central passage and opened fire. Donovan dropped flat to the deck as hot lead slugs ricocheted all around him. He was pinned and couldn't move.

He tried to formulate a plan, but didn't have time to think. From the dark storeroom to his left, a single man launched into the air, a knife raised high, and lunged at him from the darkness.

"Ah!" the man shouted as he sliced across Donovan's torso, cutting the chest sling and causing his M4 to hit the ground.

Feet skidding on the sand that covered the entrance of the cave, Miller fired a three-round burst at a Taliban soldier coming up the main pathway.

THWOOP! THWOOP! THWOOP

Once outside, he could hear the distant sounds of rotor blades approaching from the north. Miller looked over at Kaili who was exiting. Williams was close behind, but Donovan was missing!

"Where's the commander?!" Miller yelled over the sounds of gunfire.

"He was right behind us!" Kaili answered as he looked back into the darkness of the cave.

"We've got about five minutes before this entire place goes up like Hiroshima!" Miller said, pointing to the sky.

He looked back into the abyss that he'd just fought his way out of, and then back at his teammates. Miller knew what he had to do. He dropped the magazine out of his M4 and reached into his vest for a fresh one.

Suddenly, over the top of the farthest ridgeline, Miller could make out the silhouette of the Seahawk chopper coming to rescue them.

"That's our ride! Get Hassan there!" Miller yelled as he reloaded his weapon.

"What about you?" Kaili asked.

"Don't wait! Go!" Miller yelled, running into the cave.

Inside, Donovan rocketed forward with a left hook. Though his fist flew wide and failed to make contact, the shattered fragments of glass on his watch caught the man. The glass sliced through the skin on his face.

The pain, cutting through his cheek and eye socket, made him scream out and drop his knife. Donovan dropped down, rolled, grabbed his weapon, and came up firing. One shot was all he needed. The bullet hit its mark.

Bullets continued to rain down on him as the other men approached from below. A sharp pain unexpectedly bit into his leg. He looked down and saw that one of the rebounds had pierced his thigh.

Donovan's leg gave out as he reached for the wound.

Ten more soldiers poured into the chamber as he dragged himself into the relative safety of the storeroom. He placed his weapon around the corner and pulled the trigger. Amazingly, three more Taliban soldiers went down hard. The others took cover. Finally, Donovan's ammo ran dry, and he dropped his weapon.

There was a moment of peaceful calm as all firing in the cave stopped. No one was sure what was going on. Had they done it? Had they killed him? Had they destroyed the American infidel?

One of the terrorists stood and looked around the corner of the center passageway, only to be met by a .45 caliber bullet from an MK23. He fell backward and the others again opened fire.

Knowing he only had four rounds left in his pistol, Donovan chose his shots carefully. Blood spilled from his leg.

Then Donovan heard a familiar voice, yelling out behind him over the ruckus.

"Sir!" Miller yelled as he braved the onslaught of enemy lead.

Confused, Donovan looked back toward the front of the cave. Miller, M4 in the air, was laying down covering fire, trying to reach him.

Waving his hand in the air, Donovan shouted for him to get back.

"Get outta here! Get to the chopper!" Donovan ordered.

Ten more men flooded into the main passageway. There were now seventeen Taliban soldiers advancing on them and the stone could only take so much abuse before their natural cover would be gone.

"I'm hit! I can't make it! Blow the C4 and go!" Donovan ordered as he fired off the last of his rounds.

Miller didn't obey. He managed to get to Donovan's position. Once there, he smiled and handed his commander a magazine ammo for his machine gun.

"SEAL Team. We're here to get you out," Miller said with a grin.

Donovan said, "I told you to go!"

Reaching down, Miller took Donovan into a fireman's carry. Miller could move faster if his hands were free, but that would mean Donovan would have to provide covering fire.

"You said we all go home! Leave no man behind!" Miller said.

They broke cover, launching into the hail of bullets that flew between them and the exit to the cave.

An M4 in each fist, Donovan yelled bloody murder as he depressed the trigger on each weapon, firing fully automatic bursts at the enemy!

Several of the shots were true to their targets. Taliban terrorists dropped like marionettes with clipped strings and hit the deck in clumps of flesh. This was just enough cover for the men to get a head start on the enemy. Miller ran up the grade toward the exit fifty yards away.

Finally, with M4s dry and nothing to hold back the tidal wave of men, the enemy rose from their hiding spots and began to advance on the pair.

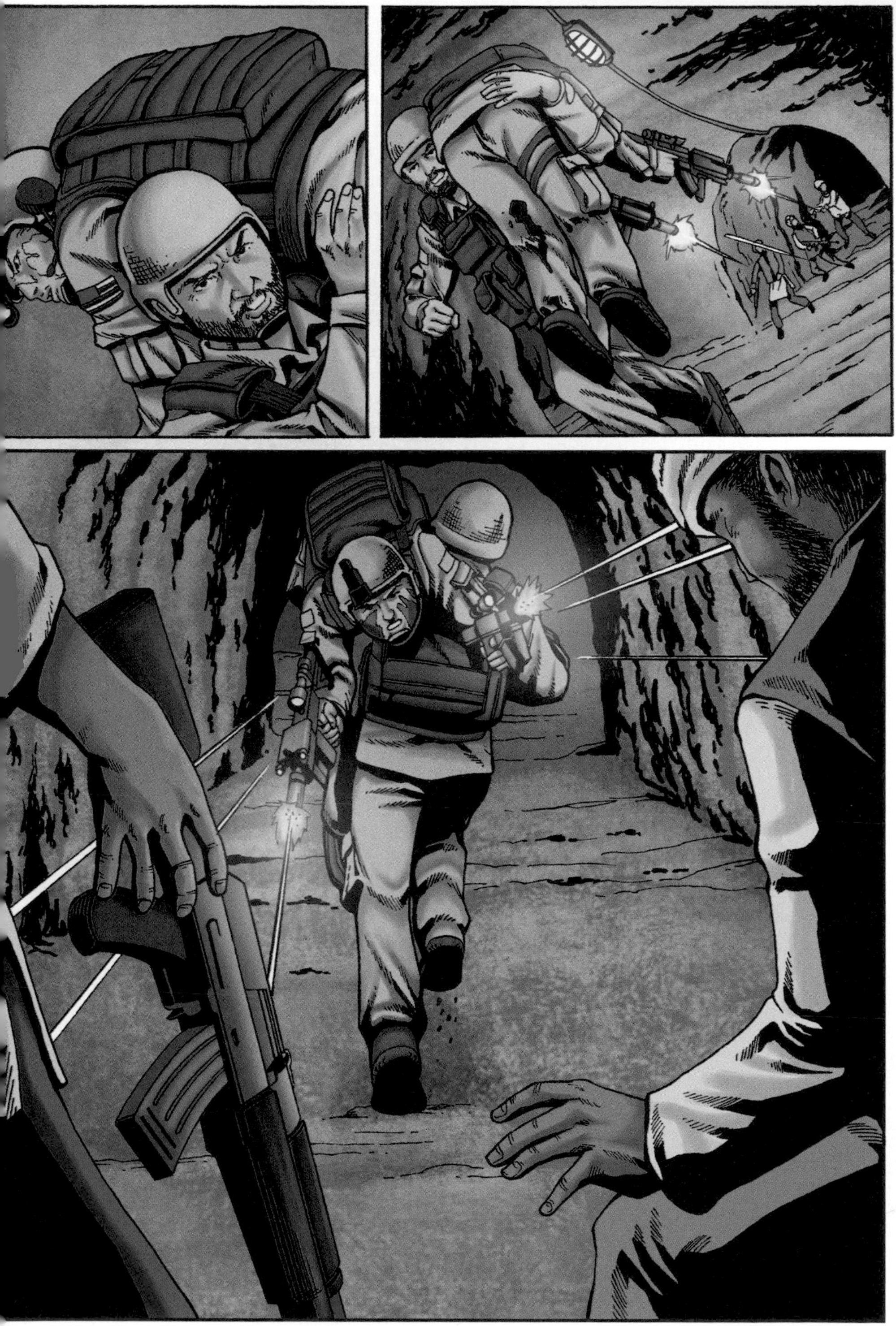

The SEALs inched closer to the mouth of the cave. Sunlight began to creep across Donovan's face. He looked forward hopefully, but the bullets that zipped past their heads reminded him they weren't home free yet. When he looked back, he saw the wall of Taliban soldiers bearing down on them.

As they made it to the mouth of the cave, Miller reached down and pulled the detonator from his pocket.

"Now, Miller!" Donovan screamed.

Miller closed his eyes and prayed as his thumb pressed the button.

BOOOM!

The earth trembled. Detonators fired and ignited the C4 plastic explosive. In a huge flash, the front of the cave filled with smoke. Loose rock and debris fell on top of the Taliban pursuers.

The shockwave reverberated outward, smacking Miller in the back, making him lose his footing. Tumbling, he dropped Donovan to the deck and rolled onto the dirt.

Quickly, Miller rose and grabbed his chief officer. The sound of jet engines filled the skies above them.

"Sir, we're not out of this yet!" Miller said. He picked up his wounded teammate and helped him to run.

Mere minutes later, as Miller and Donovan reached a relative safe distance, the Seahawk swooped in. Kaili helped the wounded commander into the bird as Miller leapt up and pulled himself in.

"Thirty seconds to impact!" the crew chief yelled. The bird lifted off the ground as quickly as it had landed. Miller's feet were still dangling out the main hatch as it rose into the air.

A single bunker buster bomb fell from the skies, digging almost 75 feet into the ground before exploding. The hillside erupted in flames.

Massive chunks of dirt and debris flew hundreds of feet into the air. The explosion shook the ground hard, the shock waves rushing through the underground maze. The entire terrorist hideout and its infrastructure were completely destroyed.

As the Seahawk helicopter flew across the desert toward base, a corpsman worked on patching up Donovan's leg. Luckily, the wound was a through and through, meaning it had gone straight through the muscle without damaging any vital systems. It would heal without permanent damage.

Donovan thought back to the crash in the helicopter.

His first thoughts after the crash had been for his men, not the mission. Would his grandfather have acted the same in Korea? His father in Vietnam? He was so worried about the safety of SEALs all over the world, he didn't even care that Hassan had escaped. Even when he was placed aboard the evac, he had asked about his teammates and demanded the corpsman deal with them first.

Williams and Kaili were going to make it through just fine. Seemed Williams had caught walking pneumonia and the specific blend of Taliban hospitality hadn't done much for it, but he'd pull through okay. And Kaili would bounce back quickly, his wounds being mostly superficial, but they'd keep him on light duty for about five weeks.

Though he was happy to hear it, Donovan was saddened by the thought of losing an entire fire-team of SEALs. *His* SEALs. Men he was personally responsible for. It felt devastating to him.

The surviving members of his team were worse for the wear, but they were alive, and that was all that mattered in the long run.

Lying back against the chopper's bulkhead, Donovan sat, his eyes closed, feeling the vibrations of the bird moving beneath him.

Under his breath, he mumbled, "I was supposed to be a poet. . . ."

Next to him, Miller frowned. "What was that, sir?" he asked.

"Nothing," Donovan replied. "Well, it's something Thomas Jefferson said: 'I was a soldier so that my son could be a farmer so that his son could be a poet.' My father said our family had given enough blood for our country and I didn't have anything to prove. But I told him there was too much injustice in the world and I was needed as a soldier, not as a poet."

A moment of silence passed as Donovan looked down at his leg and frowned. "Maybe I was wrong."

"Sir —" Miller began. He reached over and placed his hand into Donovan's cargo pocket. He retrieved the Afghani map he'd taken from the caves and handed it to his commanding officer.

"I wouldn't be here and neither would any of these guys, if it weren't for your great leadership out there today, sir," Miller said.

Donovan raised an eyebrow and looked at the master chief.

"And that yahoo," Miller went on, pointing over at Hassan, who was zip-tied and strapped into a jumper seat, still unconscious. "He would still be out there killing innocent civilians. So I'd say your father was dead wrong."

Donovan nodded. "Thanks," he said.

"Besides, sir, looks to me like you got both sides of the equation right," said Miller.

He nodded out the open door.

Leaning over, Donovan glanced out the hatch. The warm wind slapped sand at his face. Behind them, the remnants of the smoldering mountainside drifted high into the air.

"Me, I'd call that poetic justice," Miller quipped.

They both laughed as Donovan slapped the Chief on the back.

"Hooyah, Master Chief! Hooyah!" Donovan said.

DEBRIEFING

BATTLE CONDITIONS

TERRAIN

Located in southern Asia, Afghanistan is bordered by China, Iran, Pakistan, Tajikistan, Turkmenistan, and Uzbekistan. It is a landlocked nation with very little water. Nearly half of the land is considered mountainous. The Hindu Kush mountain range cuts through the country from northeast to southwest. The highest peaks in this range reach almost 23,000 feet into the air, making transportation nearly impossible, cutting off the northern section of Afghanistan from the south, and making Taliban hideouts often difficult to locate.

WEATHER

The weather in Afghanistan varies widely from one area of the nation to another. Typically, the country experiences dry summers and cold winters. However, higher elevation areas, such as the Hindu Kush mountains, can experience subzero temperatures in the winter. On the other hand, the southern plateau region of Afghanistan can become very hot and windy during the summer months. These extremes, and the overall lack of precipitation, make high-tech and adaptable clothing and gear a battlefield necessity.

THE FUTURE

SUCCESSES

Since 2001, U.S. troops have successfully overthrown the Taliban government and taken out several top Al-Qaeda leaders. Their efforts, and the support of countries around the world, have led to a new Afghan constitution and elections. To ensure the government can continue to defend themselves against the Taliban, U.S. soldiers have trained Afghan forces in security and combat techniques. In the years to come, the United States plans to help Afghanistan become a peaceful and successful nation.

WANTED

More than ten years after the 9/11 terrorist attacks, the Al-Qaeda leader Osama bin Laden remains at large. He is still on the Federal Bureau of Investigation's Ten Most Wanted List, and the U.S. Department of State is offering a $25-million reward for information leading to his capture. Since 2001, Bin Laden has sent dozens of messages to his followers, but his whereabouts remain a mystery.

EXTRAS

THE DONOVAN FAMILY

Like many real-life soldiers, the Donovan family has a history of military service. Trace their courage, tradition, and loyalty through the ages, and read other stories of these American heroes.

Renee Woodsworth
1925-1988

Michael Donovan
1926-1979

Military Rank: PFC
World War II
featured in *A Time for War*

Robert Donovan
1907-1956

Richard Lemke
1933-2001

Lillian Garvey
1905-1941

Mary Ann Donovan
1929-1988

Marcy Jacobson
1918-1941

Everett Donovan
1932-1951

Military Rank: CAPT
Korean War
featured in *Blood Brotherhood*

John Donovan
1946-2010

Harriet Winslow
1949-present

Tamara Donovan
1948-1965

Steven Donovan
1952-present

Terry Donovan
1971-present

Elizabeth Jackson
1973-present

Robert Donovan
1976-present

Katherine Donovan
1980-present

Michael Lemke
1954-present

Jacqueline Kriesel
1954-present

Donald Lemke
1978-present

Amy Jordan
1984-present

Verner Donovan
1951-present
-
Military Rank: LT
War in Vietnam
featured in *Fighting Phantoms*

Jenny Dahl
1953-2004

Lester Donovan
1972-present

Military Rank: LCDR
War in Afghanistan
featured in *Control Under Fire*

EXTRAS

ABOUT THE AUTHOR

M. ZACHARY SHERMAN is a veteran of the United States Marine Corps. He has written comics for Marvel, Radical, Image, and Dark Horse. His recent work includes *America's Army: The Graphic Novel*, *Earp: Saint for Sinners*, and the second book in the SOCOM: SEAL Team Seven trilogy.

AUTHOR Q&A

Q: Any relation to the Civil War Union General William Tecumseh Sherman?

A: Yes, indeed! I was one of the only members of my family lineage to not have some kind of active duty military participation – until I joined the U.S. Marines at age 28.

Q: Why did you decide to join the U.S. Marine Corps? How did the experience change you?

A: I had been working at the same job for a while when I thought I needed to start giving back. The biggest change for me was the ability to see something greater than myself; I got a real sense of the world going on outside of just my immediate, selfish surroundings. The Marines helped me to grow up a lot. They taught me the focus and discipline that helped get me where I am today.

Q: When did you decide to become a writer?

A: I've been writing all my life, but the first professional gig I ever had was a screenplay for Illya Salkind (*Superman* 1-3) back in 1995. But it was a secondary profession, with small assignments here and there, and it wasn't until around 2005 that I began to get serious.

Q: Has your military experience affected your writing?

A: Absolutely, especially the discipline I have obtained. Time management is key when working on projects, so you must be able to govern yourself. In regards to story, I've met and been with many different people, which enabled me to become a better storyteller through character.

Q: Describe your approach to the Bloodlines series. Did personal experiences in the military influence the stories?

A: Yes and no. I didn't have these types of experiences in the military, but the characters are based on real people I've encountered. And those scenarios are all real, just the characters we follow have been inserted into the time lines. I wanted the stories to fit into real history, real battles, but have characters we may not have heard of be the focus of those stories. I've tried to retell the truth of the battle with a small change in the players.

Q: Any future plans for the Bloodlines series?

A: There are so many battles through history that people don't know about. If they hadn't happened, the world would be a much different place! It's important to hear about these events. If we can learn from history, we can sidestep the mistakes we've made as we move forward.

ABOUT THE ILLUSTRATOR

FRITZ CASAS is a freelance illustrator for the internationally renowned creative studio Glass House Graphics, Inc. He lives in Manila, Philippines, where he enjoys watching movies, gaming, and playing his guitar.

A CALL TO ACTION

WORLD WAR II

BLOODLINES
A TIME FOR WAR

M. ZACHARY SHERMAN

KOREAN WAR

BLOODLINES
BLOOD BROTHERHOOD

M. ZACHARY SHERMAN

On June 6, 1944, Private First Class Michael Donovan and 13,000 U.S. Paratroopers fly toward their Drop Zone in enemy-occupied France. Their mission: capture the town of Carentan from the Germans and secure an operations base for Allied forces. Suddenly, the sky explodes, and their C-47 Skytrain is hit with anti-aircraft fire! Within moments, the troops exit the plane and plummet toward a deadly destination. On the ground, Donovan finds himself alone in the lion's den without a weapon. In order to survive, the rookie soldier must rely on his instincts and locate his platoon before time runs out.

On December 1, 1950, during the heart of the Korean War, Lieutenant Everett Donovan awakens in a mortar crater behind enemy lines. During the Battle of Chosin Reservoir, a mine explosion has killed his entire platoon of U.S. Marines. Shaken and shivering from the subzero temps, the lieutenant struggles to his feet and stands among the bodies of his fellow Devil Dogs. Suddenly, a shot rings out! Donovan falls to his knees and when he looks up, he's face to face with his Korean counterpart. Both men know the standoff will end in brotherhood or blood — and neither choice will come easy.

VIETNAM WAR

BLOODLINES
FIGHTING PHANTOMS

M. ZACHARY SHERMAN

AFGHANISTAN

BLOODLINES
CONTROL UNDER FIRE

M. ZACHARY SHERMAN

In late 1970, Lieutenant Verner Donovan sits aboard an aircraft carrier, waiting to fly his F-4 Phantom II over Vietnam. He's the lead roll for the next hop and eager to help the U.S. troops on the ground. Suddenly, the call comes in – a Marine unit requires air support! Within moments, Donovan and other pilots are in their birds and into the skies. Soon, however, a dogfight with MiG fighter planes takes a turn for the worse, and the lieutenant ejects over enemy territory. His copilot is injured in the fall, and Donovan must make a difficult decision: to save his friend, he must first leave him behind.

Technology and air superiority equals success in modern warfare. But even during the War in Afghanistan, satellite recon and smart bombs cannot replace soldiers on the ground. When a SEAL team Seahawk helicopter goes down in the icy mountains of Kandahar, Lieutenant Commander Lester Donovan must make a difficult decision: follow orders or go "off mission" and save his fellow soldiers. With Taliban terrorists at every turn, neither decision will be easy. He'll need his instincts and some high-tech weaponry to get off of the hillside and back to base alive!

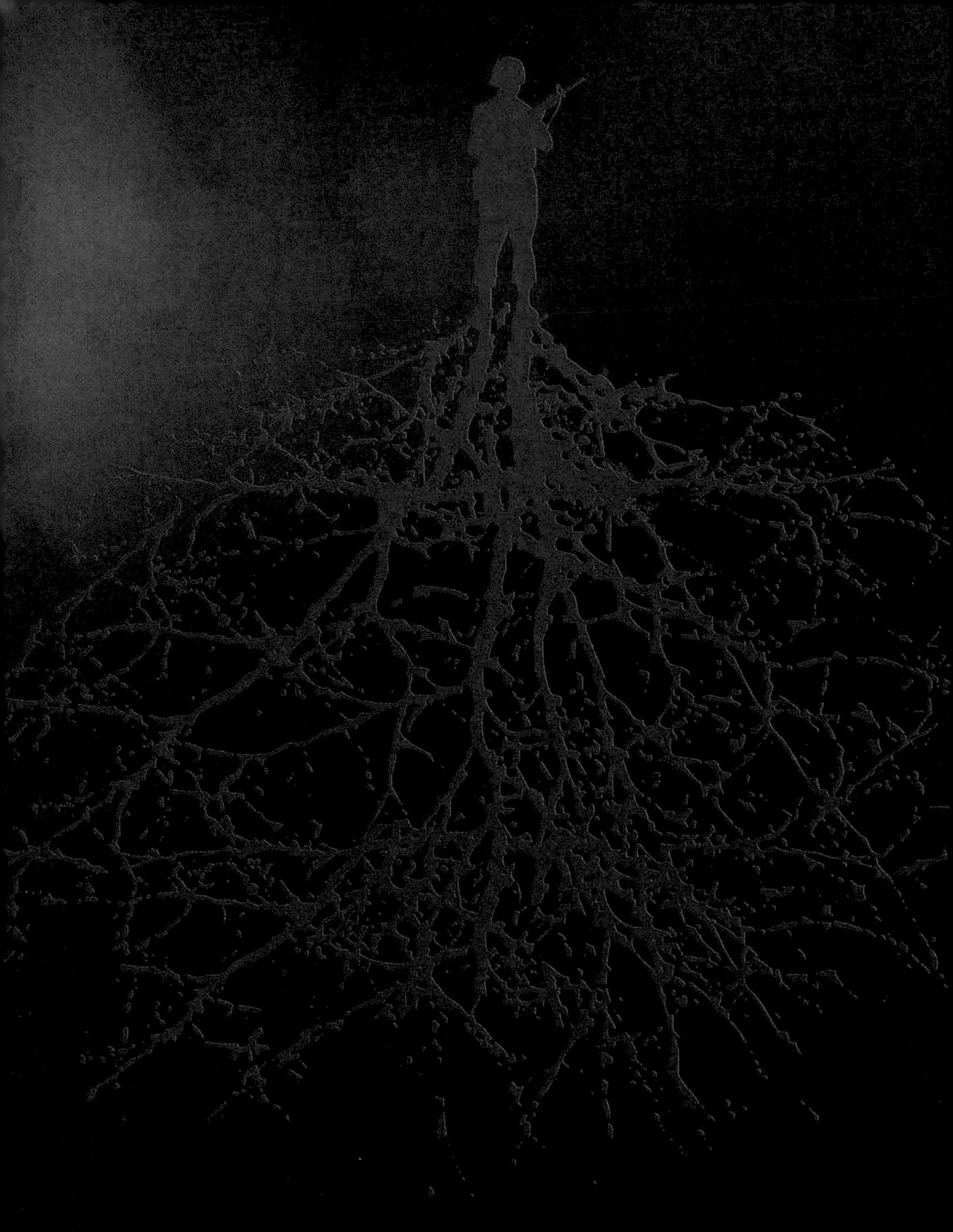

BLOODLINES

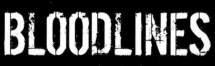

www.capstonepub.com

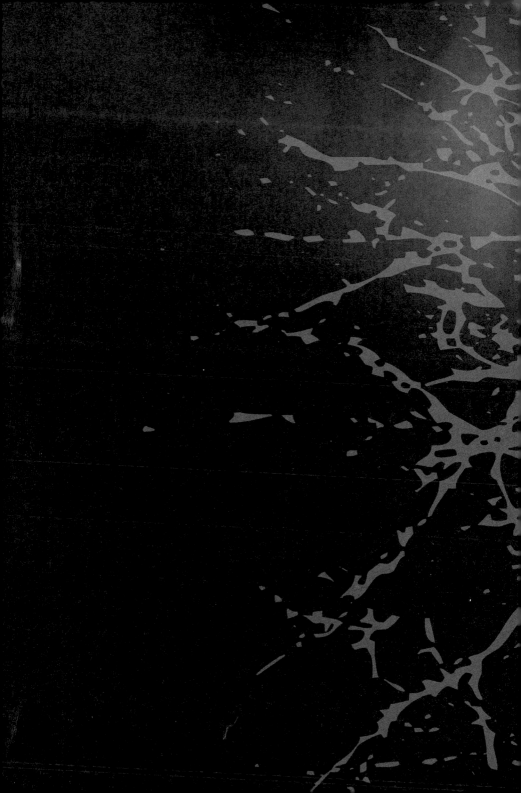

SHERM   HPLEX
Sherman, M. Zachary.
Control under fire /

PLEASANTVILLE   Houston Public Library
10/11